The Mysterious Case of an Amish Runaway

Hannah Schrock

Prologue

Millersburg, Ohio, three years earlier...

Elizabeth Lantz, Eliza to her friends, felt like she'd just doused the oil lantern in her bedroom and closed her eyes when the sound of something woke her up. She had a ground floor room in the small farmhouse she shared with her parents, while their bedroom was located on the second story, at the other end of the haus.

She opened her eyes and blinked sleepily, trying to locate the direction the sound was coming from when she realized it was coming from the window.

She quickly lit the lamp again and slipped out of bed, the coolness of the wooden floorboards making her bare toes curl. She carefully pushed the curtains aside and then gasped. Ivy Troyer, her best friend, stood outside her window looking harried. Eliza had just turned eighteen and Ivy had just turned twenty. Eliza had just finished school last year, with Ivy only a few years ahead of her.

Eliza set the lamp down and then pushed the curtain wide, unlocking the window and stepping back as Ivy tossed a brown suitcase, with a bright pink scarf tied around the handle, through the window, and then followed closely behind.

Eliza moved the suitcase to the side and hugged her friend, "What are you doing here?" Her question was whispered, even though there was no way her parents would hear them.

"I came to say goodbye," Ivy told her, the evidence of tears on her cheeks.

"Why have you been crying?" Eliza wanted to know. "And what do you mean 'goodbye'?"

"Eliza, I'm leaving Millersburg. I've tried to be happy living the Amish lifestyle, but …I want to live like the Englisch do."

"Ivy! No! You don't mean that, do you?" Eliza asked her friend, searching her eyes for the truth.

Ivy nodded her head, "I really do mean it. I can't stay here another day. I don't want this to be a big fight, that's why I'm leaving like this. And I don't want you to worry about me. I'm going to be okay."

"Maybe you should reconsider this action. You're talking about running away."

"I know, but it's the only way I'll ever be able to live…"

Eliza shook her head, pleading with her friend, "You know, you could talk to Minister Miller, maybe get another opinion and some more options…?"

Ivy frantically shook her head, "No! I'm leaving tonight, I just wanted to see you to say goodbye." Ivy reached for her suitcase and started to push it back through the window, "You're the only person I'll really miss around here."

"But…what about your parents? They'll be so worried…"

Ivy gave her a smile, "I left them a letter telling them I was going to live with the Englisch. They won't understand. I asked them not to look for me, but to let me get settled and then I would find a way to contact them. I don't want you to look for me either. Don't cause trouble for yourself, just let me go and know this is what I want."

She looked sad for a moment and Eliza voiced what she thought was the reason, "You know once you leave they won't be allowed to have any contact with you. None of us will. Don't you?"

Ivy nodded sadly, "Yes, and it breaks my heart to think I'll never see them again, but I can't stay here and be unhappy for the rest of my life. I need to leave."

Eliza stared at the friend she'd known since they were toddlers. "I can't believe I might never see you again." She felt tears threaten to spill over her eyes, "Are you sure this is what you want to do?"

"It's what I need to do," Ivy replied, hugging her close for a moment before pushing the suitcase through the window and climbing out after it. "I'll never forget you, Eliza. You're the best friend a person could ever ask for."

Eliza watched as Ivy picked up the suitcase, the pink scarf flapping in the breeze as she hurried towards the road. Eliza wanted to call after her, but she knew that nothing she could say would change her friend's mind. Ivy was stubborn and had decided to leave the Amish community where she'd been born and raised. Eliza couldn't imagine ever leaving Millersburg, but she couldn't find fault in Ivy following her own dreams.

If Ivy needed to live among the Englisch in order to be happy, she wished her well. She stared after her friend's retreating back until she could no longer see her. Then she shut the window and curtains, doused the lamp and climbed back in bed. She offered up a silent prayer to Gott that her friend would find what she was looking for and not lose sight of everything she'd been brought up to believe. She hoped Ivy found happiness and would one day find a way to let her friends and family know she was doing okay.

The Shocking Discovery

Four years later, mid-June, Millersburg, Ohio...

Thomas Schwartz walked towards the lake, his heart as heavy as the burden he carried in his arms. His beloved dog, Blue. Blue had been his canine friend since Thomas was six years old, but he'd been going downhill for the last few months, and had finally taken his last breath only hours earlier.

It was midday, and as Thomas gazed towards the river, he wished with all of his heart that he was coming here to relax and fish. But today, his reason for coming to the river was anything but relaxing.

Reaching the spot he'd chosen in his mind to lay his beloved dog to rest, he set the bundle down and pulled the shovel from his backpack. He pulled the jar of water from inside the pack and took a long drink, wiping the sweat off his brow with the rolled up sleeve of his shirt.

Putting the empty jar down, he picked up the shovel and began to dig. He recited Bible verses as he did so, taking comfort in the Scriptures he'd been taught from the time he could remember. At the age of twenty-two, he'd already made his decision to remain part of the Amish community where he'd been born. Leaving had never really crossed his mind.

He knew some people were curious as to why he wasn't actively trying to find a wife, but so far none of them had openly questioned his reasons. Thomas believed the Gott had someone special in mind for him, and that there was a perfect time for him to meet this person. He even acknowledged that his future wife could be someone he was already acquainted with, and the timing just wasn't right yet.

His mind continued to roam as he went through the physical action of removing soil from the grave he was digging. When his shovel hit something bulky and hard, he put a little more effort behind the shovel, but the resistance only seemed to increase.

He pulled the shovel out of the hole, now approximately three feet deep and three feet wide, and he gazed down, expecting to see a large boulder or tree trunk impeding his progress. Instead, he saw what appeared to be a handle, attached with metal brackets to some kind of fabric.

He squatted down on his knees and reached for the handle, tugging with all of his might until the object finally came free and he fell backwards, landing in the softened dirt. The object came out of the hole, and he was surprised to see it was a suitcase. He brushed some of the dirt off of it and realized it was a brown fabric material, and a pink piece of fabric was tied around the corner of the handle.

He picked it up and carried it a short distance away and fiddled with the lock until it finally gave way. He opened the case, and was surprised to see it contained clothing, shoes, pictures, and a few books.

Most of the stuff inside was water-stained, but as he sorted through the contents, he could still clearly make out the images on the pictures. He was even more surprised to see images of people he knew on the pictures. Ivy Troyer was pictured in several of them, and in one, she was seen smiling with her arm around Eliza Lantz.

Knowing that both girls had been raised in the same community as himself, he was surprised to see such photos in the case. The Amish typically abhorred pictures, thinking them prideful and lending towards an misplaced ego. He gazed at the pictures and realized that they had to have been taken while the girls were in the Englisch town.

After looking at everything, he put it all back in the suitcase and closed the lid. He couldn't remember seeing Ivy Troyer in years, and barely remembered her. But Eliza Lantz was a girl he saw quite regularly. They weren't friends by any stretch of the imagination, but they were polite to one another in passing.

He brought an image of Eliza to his mind and smiled. She was a pretty girl, seemed very smart and he'd never seen her be anything less than charming to those around her. He recalled that she and Ivy had been best friends as young girls, and then bits and pieces of the past came back to his memory. Ivy Troyer had run away, leaving only a note for her parents saying she wanted to live like the Englisch, and he remembered Eliza had been very upset by her friend's disappearance. Ivy had left Millersburg, and abandoned her friendship with Eliza at the same time.

He brushed at the suitcase, noticing how stained it was in places and wondering how it had ended up buried in the mud next to the river. As he rubbed at the caked mud on the surface, he suddenly realized that some of the stains were darker than the others and didn't want to rub off. The mud and dirt could be flaked off with his fingers, but beneath the mud, there appeared to be stains left behind by something that had soaked into the fabric.

He turned his attention to the pink scrap of fabric, only to realize it was a girl's headscarf. The dirt flaked off as well, and that's when he realized it was stained just like the suitcase. But the stains on the scarf weren't just dark, they were dark red. Like dried blood.

Thomas dropped his hands, rubbing them on the legs of his dark trousers as he realized the stains on the suitcase were probably dried blood as well. What happened here to leave this much blood behind?

His mind in a flurry, he abandoned the suitcase and finished the act of burying Blue. He said a quick thank you for all of the happy memories he and the dog had shared and then he turned his attention back to the suitcase. He needed to do something with it, but what?

I could take it to Ivy's parents. But then he discarded that idea. He recalled seeing them around town and at the monthly church services, depressed and heartbroken over their daughter's disappearance.

So, if not her parents, then who? He recalled the pictures and decided he would take the suitcase to Eliza. If she thought Ivy's parents could handle knowing about the suitcase, he'd trust her judgment.

He tucked his shovel back into his backpack, picked up the stained suitcase, and began the long walk back to town. Along the way, his mind worked overtime as he tried to imagine the mystery the suitcase held. Ivy had, by her own letter, runaway. But her suitcase had been found buried next to the river. What could have happened that would have caused Ivy to leave behind her clothing, memories, and even her Bible?

Thomas hoped Eliza would have some answers. He went straight to her home once he arrived back in town. Her father was in the field, and Thomas waved a greeting to him as he approached the farmhouse.

Eliza was outside, tending to the small garden and watched him with open curiosity as he walked towards her, the suitcase in his hand. "Good afternoon, Eliza."

"Good afternoon, Thomas. What brings you out here?" Eliza asked, surprised by his appearance. His dark hair was mussed, there were mud stains all over his trousers, and his shirt sleeves were rolled up and stained with mud and water.

Thomas lifted the object in his hand and Eliza's eyes followed it. When he drew close enough for her to truly see what he held, she gasped and covered her mouth with her hand. "Where did you get that?"

Thomas watched her and then set the case down between them, "I found it buried next to the river."

Eliza looked up at him, "The river? What were you doing down by the river?"

Thomas got a sad look on his face and then softly replied, "Burying my dog, Blue. This was buried about three feet down."

"I'm sorry about your dog." Eliza looked at him, and then as if she had no other choice, her eyes fixed on the suitcase. "I don't understand."

"Don't understand what?" Thomas asked, confused by the sad look on her face and the tears that she was trying not to shed.

"Why Ivy's suitcase would be buried by the river. And why did you bring it to me?" Eliza asked him.

"You're positive this is Ivy Troyer's suitcase?" he asked in response to her questions.

Eliza nodded, "Yes, the same one she had with her the night she ran away. The pink scarf was even tied around the handle that night." Eliza covered her mouth with her hand, and Thomas didn't miss the fact that it was shaking slightly.

Ignoring her response, he told her, "I opened it up and found several pictures inside, one of them showed you and Ivy smiling. There are some clothes, shoes, and a few books."

"But why bring it to me? Why not take it to her parents? I can tell you how to find their haus."

"I thought about that, but then I started to clean the mud off and discovered it's stained. With blood. Lots of blood," Thomas showed her the stains on the suitcase and scarf.

"Blood? Nee! Why would it be covered in blood?" Eliza asked. "Maybe it's not really Ivy's suitcase..." Her tears were flowing freely now, and she collapsed on the grass next to the suitcase, laying one hand upon the top of it. Almost reverently.

"Open it up and see for yourself," Thomas suggested.

Eliza nodded and sat the suitcase down on the grass, popping the latch and throwing back the lid. She picked up the clothing articles and fresh tears ran down her cheeks. These were definitely Ivy's clothing, and her pictures and even her Bible. "It's hers."

Thomas had squatted down next to her and met her eyes, "I wasn't sure if her parents could handle this or not."

Eliza nodded her understanding, "I believe they can. They were so distraught when they discovered what she'd done. They'd even gone to the police for help, but the police informed them that as she was twenty, she was an adult and could choose where she wanted to live."

She met his gaze and added, "It broke their hearts when the police refused to help track their daughter down. I was angry with her for the longest time, putting her parents through so much heartache. She told me she'd written to them, and I believe she thought the letters would give them peace, but the exact opposite was the case. They couldn't understand why she would decide to leave them so suddenly. Her mother was ill with headaches for months afterwards."

Thomas nodded his head, "I can imagine they were in complete shock."

"As was I. I urged her to reconsider the night she left, but she had her mind made up."

Thomas nodded his head and then stood up, "So, what do you think I should do with the suitcase?"

Eliza stood up as well, smoothing down her apron and wishing she could take her eyes off of the bloodstained suitcase. "I think her parents need to be aware that the suitcase was found so that they can contact the police again. Maybe this time, the police will act and try to find out what happened to Ivy. Her

parents deserve to have some peace where
their daughter is concerned."

An Investigation Begins

Eliza and Thomas arrived at the Troyer haus an hour later. Eliza had borrowed her daed's buggy, since Thomas had arrived on foot. He'd insisted on accompanying her, and given how emotional seeing Ivy's suitcase had left her, she was relieved to have some company.

Emma Troyer, Ivy's mamm was sitting on the front porch shelling the season's first peas and she gave Eliza a curious look, only darting a quick look towards Thomas before turning her attention back to the young girl who had once been her daughter's best friend.

"Frau Troyer, is your husband nearby?" Eliza asked her softly.

Emma nodded her head and pointed towards the barn, "He just came in from the fields. Did you need to see him?"

"Actually, I would like to speak with you both."

Thomas stepped up and informed them both quietly, "I'll go get him."

Eliza gave him a thankful smile and then joined Emma on the porch. "May I help you?"

Emma nodded and pushed the bowl to the middle of the small table between the two chairs. They worked in silence until Thomas returned with Ivy's daed by his side. Eliza wiped her hands on her apron and stood up to greet him. "Herr Troyer. I'm sorry to disturb your work."

"I was finished for the day child. What brings you here?"

Eliza gestured towards the chair she'd just vacated, "I wanted to speak with you both about something Thomas found earlier today. Have you met Thomas Schwartz?"

Ivy's daed, Matthew, nodded and then quietly introduced Emma to Thomas. When finished, he sat down and then looked between Eliza and Thomas. "What did you find?"

Thomas looked at Eliza, and when she nodded her head, he returned to the buggy and carried the stained suitcase back to the porch. When the Troyer's recognized what he held in his hands, Emma burst into noisy tears, and Matthew's face lost all color as he surged to his feet.

"Where did you find that again?" Matthew asked hoarsely.

"Thomas found it buried next to the river."

"The river?! Why would Ivy's suitcase have been by the river?"

Eliza swallowed back her own tears. The mystery of Ivy's quick departure from their Ordnung had suddenly been brought back to the forefront, as had all of the emotions surrounding her leaving.

Matthew placed a comforting arm around Emma, whispering quietly to her as she buried her head in his chest and wept. "Did you open it?" he asked, his voice indicating a chance that maybe it wasn't actually Ivy's suitcase.

Eliza nodded, "Ja. It is definitely Ivy's. Herr Troyer, I can see how upsetting this is for you, but I need you to look at the suitcase carefully for a moment."

Matthew released Emma and did as Eliza asked, immediately noticing the staining. "What are those?"

Thomas spoke up for the first time, "I'm sorry, but those stains appear to be dried blood. I think I can speak for Eliza when I say that she, and I, am very worried that something bad happened to your daughter."

"I really think you should contact the authorities again," Eliza told everyone. She couldn't shake the feeling that something had happened to Ivy. The stains on the suitcase were large, and she had a hard time not allowing her mind to run away with thoughts of the types of injuries Ivy must have suffered to leave behind that much blood. Provided that the blood was indeed Ivy's. there was always the possibility that it was someone else's blood.

Thomas offered to take walk with Matthew to the emergency phone at the end of the street. While their Ordnung didn't believe in using modern conveniences, they did believe in being safe. As those that didn't understand their way of life became more curious, they had also become more dangerous. It had become necessary to provide a way for everyone to seek the help of the Englisch police at those times, so emergency phones had been installed along the main roads for just such a purpose.

Eliza helped Emma into the house and fixed her a cup of coffee, hoping the warm drink would help ease her sorrow. It was like losing Ivy all over again, and Eliza couldn't turn her mind off. She'd spent many nights wishing she'd done more to keep her friend from leaving Millersburg that last night, and now she found herself right back in that mindset.

If only I'd found a way to make her stay, maybe…

"Eliza," Emma spoke to her firmly, sitting up straighter in her chair. "You can't go blaming yourself. Whatever happened that took Ivy away from here, we can't undo it."

Eliza nodded and wiped her cheeks with her fingers, "I know that, but sometimes it's hard to get one's mind to acknowledge that truth."

"Ja, I know. Hopefully the police will be more helpful this time."

Eliza nodded her head, and decided that whether or not the police wanted to help solve the mystery of the stained suitcase, she needed to learn the truth about what happened to her friend. She would start asking around and see what information she could find out. The Amish were wary of most Englisch and just because they wore a uniform, didn't change that much. They would be hesitant to speak to a uniformed officer, but maybe not to Eliza. One of their own.

The police arrived shortly after Thomas and Matthew returned to the farmhouse. They questioned Thomas extensively about the suitcase and even produced a map and asked him to point out the location of where he'd found it.

Thomas did so, while Matthew and Emma looked on. "So, how deep was the suitcase buried?"

"About three feet, give or take a few inches."

"Hmm…did you look around to see if there was anything else buried nearby?" one of the officers asked, his pen poised over his tablet.

Thomas shook his head, "No, I didn't. I moved up the bank a bit and dug another hole to bury Blue in and then brought the suitcase back to town."

"Son, we're probably going to need you to come with us and show us exactly where this all took place."

"Alright, I guess I can do that," Thomas told the man, wanting to cooperate as much as possible.

"Mr. and Mrs. Troyer, I'll have to dig up the old file from several years ago, but since I wasn't on the case back then, can you give me a quick rundown of the night your daughter disappeared."

Matthew nodded and then stated, "We didn't know anything was wrong. We ate dinner together and then she went to her room like always. It wasn't until the next morning when she didn't take care of her morning chores that Emma looked in on her and realized she wasn't there. That's when we found the note asking us to not search for her."

"So, she ran away?" the officer probed.

Eliza stepped forward, "Ivy came to see me that night…to say goodbye. She told me she wanted to go live in the Englisch world and knew her parents wouldn't understand. She told me she left them a note and asked me not to look for her, that she would be okay. She was carrying that suitcase with the pink scarf tied around the handle."

"Do you remember what time this all happened?"

"Nee, not exactly, but I'd already gone to sleep…maybe around 11 o'clock?"

"Very good." The officer closed his tablet and then spoke to the Troyer's, "I'll go through the old file and if I have any other questions I'll be in touch. In person, since you folks don't use the telephone."

"Danke, officer. Please find out what happened to our daughter," Matthew pleaded quietly.

"I'll do my best, but I have to be honest…this happened four years ago, and with the water damage on the suitcase, we might not be able to get much evidence from it. The blood stains won't do us any good unless we already have some information in our computers. Are there any medical records that might help us determine if the bloodstains on the suitcase belonged to your daughter?"

"Ja, Ivy was born at the Englisch hospital."

The officer smiled, "Excellent, that will help immensely." When he looked up at saw the hopeful looks on the Troyer's faces, he hurried to add, "that doesn't necessarily mean it will make piecing this story together any easier. We still have a lot of unanswered questions."

"We understand and will pray that Gott helps guide you to the answers," Matthew told him somberly.

The officer looked at him and then shook his head, "I'm afraid it might take an act of your Gott in order to solve this mystery. I'm sorry for your loss." He shook Matthew's hand, nodded to Emma and then excused himself from the kitchen.

Eliza looked after him, hoping that he truly did intend to start an investigation, but also doubtful that it would lead him anywhere useful. Nee, if any resolution is to be had, someone from within the Ordnung is going to need to figure it out. Might as well be me.

The Letters

Eliza turned back to the Troyer's, "I realize this has all been a shock, but I would like to help. Would it be inappropriate for me to ask to see Ivy's room?"

"Nee," Emma told her, rising and heading towards the stairs. "Nothing has been changed since the night she left."

"Nothing?" Eliza asked, curiously.

Emma sadly shook her head, "I just kept hoping she would come back. She belonged here, not with the Englisch."

Eliza didn't respond, but she followed Emma to a closed door. Emma stepped aside, "You go on in, I don't think I can right now."

"I understand." She looked up and saw that Thomas had followed them to the top of the stairs, "Would you like to help?"

Thomas allowed Emma to go back downstairs and then joined her at the opening to the room, "Is this Ivy's room?"

"It is. I'm hoping that maybe she left a clue as to why she suddenly wanted to live with the

Englisch. It took me by complete surprise to be honest."

"Won't it feel like we're trespassing to go digging through her things?" Thomas asked.

Eliza shook her head, "Nee, I don't think so. I need to know what happened to Ivy, and this room contains the only clues left of her. There has to be something here that can help."

Thomas nodded his head but didn't step inside the room, "I'll just watch then."

Eliza nodded at him, and methodically started going through the room. She started at the dresser which didn't seem to contain anything out of the ordinary. Clothes. Socks and undergarments. Ivy hadn't even taken all of her clothing with her when she left. Eliza found that somewhat odd, but then again, if Ivy had intended to live as an Englischer, she wouldn't have had any use for identical dresses, skirts, blouses, aprons, and prayer kapps.

The small table beside the bed was covered with a fine layer of dust and held an oil lamp and small wind up clock that had long since stopped counting time. There was nothing beneath the bed, leaving only the closet.

Eliza pulled open the doors and then stared at the skirts, blouses, aprons, and dresses still hanging there. The caps of the sleeves were dingy with dust that had collected, and Eliza realized that the room had been untouched since Ivy left.

"It doesn't look there's anything in the closet but clothes and shoes," Thomas commented from the doorway.

Eliza nodded her head and then pushed the hangars to one side of the closet, revealing a small set of shelves. She grinned as she pulled a small box from one of the shelves. "Not everything is as it seems."

Thomas smiled back at her and asked, "How did you know there would be something besides clothing in her closet?"

Eliza smiled, "Because I also have keepsakes and such hidden away in my closet."

"Oh!" He gestured towards the box, "What do you think is in it?"

Eliza carried it over to the bed and set it down on the quilt, coughing as a cloud of dust rose up. "There's only one way to find out." She lifted the top off and then picked up a small pile of envelopes. "It looks like letters."

Thomas's curiosity got the best of him and he stepped into the room, looking over her shoulder, "Yellowcreek? That's only a couple of miles away from Millersburg."

Eliza nodded her head, "These letters came from Mary Zook."

"Do you know who that is?" Thomas asked.

"No, but look at the postmark. These letters were all written a few weeks before Ivy left."

"Maybe they will give you some clues as to why she left?" Thomas suggested.

"Maybe." Eliza opened the first letter and read it out loud –

> Ivy,
>
> I understand you are upset, but I really feel you should tell someone in your Ordnung. I will say a prayer for you that Gott will give you wisdom in this situation.
>
> Mary

"That's pretty vague. When was that letter written?" Thomas asked.

Eliza looked at the postmark, "A week before she left." She thumbed through the rest of the letters and started putting them in order from earliest to latest. She pulled the first letter out and read it –

> Ivy,
>
> You seem very upset. I wish I were there so we could talk in person. Please know that I am here if you need a friend.
>
> What you have shared is very troubling indeed. I don't why you feel so afraid. I cannot believe that anyone would be out to harm you.
>
> Please take care and write to me again when you can.
>
> Mary

"Did you know Ivy was afraid someone was out to hurt her? It sounds like she was really scared?"

Eliza shook her head, "She never said anything to me about that." There were only two more letters, so she opened up the next one and read –

> Ivy,

You mentioned visiting me and please know that you are welcome anytime. Have you spoken with anyone regarding your concerns?

Maybe if you come to visit, you can tell me what has you so scared and together we can figure out a solution.

You mentioned hiding amongst the Englisch, please consider this carefully. The elders of my Ordnung would not be so forgiving, as I am sure yours would respond likewise. Are you positive that what you know requires this kind of sacrifice?

Mary

Eliza was confused, "It sounds like Ivy was thinking of going to live with the Englisch because she wanted to hide. But from what?"

Thomas looked at her and asked, "Or from whom? I cannot imagine anything in Millersburg causing so much fear that Ivy would want to run away. Is it possible that someone was threatening her, or maybe hurt her?"

Eliza knew what Thomas was asking and shook her head, "I don't think so. Millersburg is such a quiet village. Everyone gets along with everyone else so well."

"Or so you thought. Evidently something, or someone, had your friend scared to death."

"Let's see what the last letter says," Eliza commented, pulling the last letter out and smoothing the paper open. It was dated the day before Ivy left –

> Ivy,
>
> Of course you can come stay with me. Maybe getting some distance from this situation will help you see clearly the path that should be taken to resolve the issue.
>
> I will expect your arrival in the next day or so.
>
> Mary

"That was written the day before she left. So, maybe she only told me she was going to live with the Englisch so I wouldn't look for her, but in reality she was just going up the road a few miles and planning to live with Mary."

"Do you know this Mary Zook?"

Eliza shook her head, "No, but I think it might be time we met one another. Don't you?"

Finding Answers

Yellowcreek, the next afternoon…

Thomas had insisted on taking his own buggy to Yellowcreek, and truth be told, Eliza hadn't minded one bit. With someone else responsible for their direction and control of the horse, it left her plenty of time to consider the letter's they'd found amongst Ivy's thing the afternoon before.

After reading the letters, they'd gone back downstairs to speak with the Troyer's but Matthew had informed them that Emma had gone to bed, and he wasn't prepared to discuss the situation any further that day.

Eliza had respectfully nodded her head and told him that she would be praying for them both, and hoped that they would receive some answers and peace soon.

"How do you think Ivy became friends with Mary, being as they lived in different villages?" Thomas asked as they entered the small village.

"I really don't know, but Ivy came to Yellowcreek from time to time, they must have met on one of her visits."

"There's her house," Thomas pointed up ahead. He pulled the buggy into the small driveway and engaged the brake. "Ready?"

Eliza nodded, "Ja." She waited for Thomas to come around and help her out of the buggy, per his request, and then they walked up to the haus together. It was a small residence, located in town, and Eliza secretly wondered how old Mary was.

She knocked on the door, and a few moments later a small woman answered the door. She was dressed in a dark blue dress with the customary apron and prayer kapp in place, her dark brown hair secured beneath, leaving her face open.

"Ja?"

"We're looking for Mary Zook?" Eliza told her with a small smile.

"I am Mary Zook."

"My name is Elizabeth Lantz," she told her, and then she glanced at her companion. "And this is Thomas Schwartz. We're from

Millersburg and were wondering if we could speak with you for a few minutes?"

"Millersburg?" Mary asked, looking slightly suspicious.

"Ja. We wanted to talk to you about Ivy Troyer."

"Ivy?! You know Ivy?"

Eliza nodded her head, "She was my best friend growing up. Could we come in for a few minutes?"

Mary nodded her head and stepped back, "I met Ivy several years ago at a church gathering. She was here visiting friends and they introduced us." She smiled at the memory as she led them towards a small sitting room at the front of the small house. She gestured for them to be seated and then continued, "She and I became friends, almost like sisters."

"You were older?" Eliza asked.

Mary nodded, "A few years, I turned twenty-six this last birthday."

"Ivy would be twenty-four now," Eliza murmured.

Mary looked at her strangely and then told them, "I'm surprised to see anyone here asking about Ivy. She wrote me four years ago and was very upset. She'd seen something that truly frightened her."

Eliza looked at Thomas and then withdrew the letters from her apron pocket, "We found these letters in Ivy's closet. She mentioned being scared…did she tell you what she was afraid of?"

Mary sighed, "No, but she told me that she wanted to be away from Millersburg. She asked if she could come stay with me while she figured out what to do, and I agreed. I wanted her to talk to someone, but she was too afraid."

Mary closed her eyes for a moment, and then started speaking again, "She wrote and said that she would be arriving soon, and I wrote her back to tell her that she was welcome whenever. I truly thought I would see her in a few days, but when more than a week went by, I wrote her again. Several letters in fact, but she never answered them.

"After several weeks went by, I figured she'd decided to go live amongst the Englisch instead of with me. Her mamm wrote me about that time, asking if I knew where Ivy was. I wrote her back, telling that Ivy had been planning on coming to stay with me, but must have changed her mind. I haven't heard from anyone since then."

Mary paused and looked at both of her visitors, "Why are you here now asking about Ivy?"

Thomas spoke up, "I found a suitcase yesterday buried by the river a short distance from Millersburg. It was Ivy's."

Mary gasped and tears stung her eyes, "Ivy's suitcase…I don't understand."

Eliza nodded, "Ivy came to see me one night, four years ago. She had a brown suitcase with her, with a pink scarf tied around the handle…"

"I know that scarf. She got it here in Yellowcreek…"

"Anyway, she told me she was going to live with the Englisch, that she didn't want to live an Amish lifestyle any longer and that I shouldn't worry or look for her. She told me she left a letter stating the same thing for her daed and mamm."

"I still don't understand, she told you she was going to live with the Englisch but I thought she was coming to live with me. I guess she changed her mind…"

Eliza took a breath and then told her, "Maybe, but the suitcase was stained with blood."

Thomas added, "The authorities took it to their lab to have the blood stains analyzed. To see if it belonged to Ivy."

"That's horrible," Mary stated, clasping her hands together and looking very sad."

"Mary, did Ivy tell you anything else that might help us figure out what she'd seen or was afraid of?"

Mary shook her head, "Nee, I tried to get her to say more, but she wouldn't. She was really scared."

"We're starting to understand that."

"You don't think that something happened to her, do you? I mean, she was frightened for her life…"

Eliza sighed, "Right now, I don't know what to think. We need to figure out what she was afraid of." And since there aren't any answers to be found here in Yellowcreek, we're headed back to Millersburg. Empty handed.

Secrets

Millersburg later that same day…

Thomas dropped Eliza off in the center of town, per her request. She wanted time to think, and the walk home was the perfect way for that to happen. She waved goodbye to him, watching him drive away and thinking how nice it was to have someone helping her with this mystery.

Thomas was a very nice man, and the more time she spent in his presence, the more she liked what she saw. He was patient and compassionate, and yet he exuded an inner strength that she found very comforting.

She walked down the sidewalk and was just about to cross the street when Minister Miller stepped out of the church a few buildings up and waved her forward. Eliza immediately became agitated and nervous. He was a highly respected member of the Ordnung, a proud man, and the prospect of speaking with him was daunting.

Eliza swallowed and then continued down the sidewalk, "Minister Miller, were you signaling me?"

The man nodded and then stepped back inside the building. This Amish community was one of the few that held their worship services in a central location in town, rather than rotating around to ever changing members' homes.

"Eliza, where have you been?"

Eliza blinked at him and then slowly answered, "I was in Yellowcreek speaking with a friend of Ivy's…"

"That's what I was afraid of. As the spiritual leader of this Ordnung, I'm telling you to stop this silly investigation you've undertaken. It is agitating the villagers, especially the Troyers."

Eliza shook her head, "They deserve to know what happened to their dochder…"

"Then the police will get them those answers."

"The police didn't help last time, and they aren't doing enough now. They didn't even search her room."

"Elizabeth," he used her full name and a stern voice, "I am commanding you to stop this. Leave it to the authorities."

"Minister Miller, I don't mean to be disrespectful..."

"Then do as your told!"

Eliza was stunned, and getting angry. She'd never been confronted by so much anger, especially not from someone whom she was supposed to look up to. "Minister Miller, I don't understand why you're so angry. Please, I just want to find out what happened to Ivy...she was scared."

"How do you know she was scared? Didn't you tell everyone she came to see you the night she ran away and that she wanted to live like the Englisch?"

Eliza nodded, "That's what happened, but this friend in Yellowcreek said that Ivy told her she was scared. She'd seen something that had frightened her."

Minister Miller shook his head, his gray beard swaying with the motion and almost dislodging the black hat he wore. "I care not to know the details, that is to be left for the authorities. Now, you are to stop asking questions and leave the Troyer's to grieve in peace. I won't have anyone stirring up trouble here. Are we clear?"

Eliza was frustrated and thought of arguing further with the man, but her upbringing came into play and she nodded her head and then left the church building. She walked towards the woods, angry at the Minister's unfeeling attitude.

The Troyer's had lost a dochder and Eliza didn't see how trying to help figure out what had happened to her was a bad thing. She arrived at her familyes haus a while later, and helped her mamm finish preparing their dinner. She retired to her bedroom shortly thereafter, and tried to sleep, but it took quite a while for sleep to come.

She kept replaying the information she and Thomas had obtained from the letters and speaking with Mary Zook. Unfortunately, she didn't have any idea of where to look next. She finally fell asleep, realizing that she would just have to be patient and wait on the authorities to come up with some information from the suitcase. It was the only clue left.

*****

Late the next afternoon, Eliza looked up from where she was tending the garden to see Matthew Troyer arriving in his buggy with Emma seated beside him. He helped his fraa from the conveyance and they walked towards her as she met them halfway.

"Eliza, we wanted to come by and tell you the police stopped by earlier this morning with some preliminary results back from the lab."

Eliza nodded her head, searching both of their eyes for a clue as to what those results might have been. Emma looked terribly sad, and her eyes were red as if she'd been crying. She steeled herself to hear the worst news.

Matthew cleared his throat and then stiffened his spine, "The lab confirmed that some of the blood on the suitcase belonged to Ivy." His voice caught in his throat and he took a moment before continuing, "There was evidence of at least one other person's blood and they are trying to figure out more details now."

"More than one person's blood? Do they think Ivy was in some sort of accident then?" Eliza asked, her heart breaking as she realized her friend was more than likely dead and had been for years.

"They are not saying much else right now, just that they will be in touch. We just thought you might want to know. Ivy treasured your friendship," Matthew told her with a sad nod.

"Danke for thinking of me in this time of sorrow."

Matthew nodded once and then led his fraa back to the buggy and assisted her into it. He climbed in on the other side and drove the buggy back out onto the road. Eliza watched them leave, wishing there was a way to get more answers for them. Ivy was their only kinner, and while she'd never had any of her own, she could very well imagine the heartache that would accompany losing one. Especially under such circumstances.

She went back to her chores, her mind working furiously as she attempted to find the missing piece to the puzzle. Something that had occurred in Millersburg, or something Ivy had witnessed, had scared her to the point she felt compelled to run away. Only, she'd never made it to her destination – wherever that might have been. Something was amiss in Millersburg, but with Ivy's testimony long gone, Eliza wondered if her secrets would ever come out.

A Fraud and Sinner

Four days later...

Eliza parked her daed's buggy at the end of the street and headed for the market. Millersburg was somewhat unique in that it was a mostly Amish community, however, there were several Englisch businesses that had come to town and been granted the rights to live amongst them.

While they didn't subscribe to the non-use of technology like their Amish neighbors, they did their best to emulate the quiet, sedate lifestyle. There were several such businesses along this stretch of the village, and Eliza wasn't planning on visiting any of them today, so she wasn't paying very close attention to her surroundings.

She had just passed the butcher's shop, when suddenly she was grabbed from behind and pulled into the alley. She struggled against the hand covering her mouth and the other hand wrapped high around her shoulders, but she couldn't break the man's hold.

She knew it was a man because of his massive size.

"Hush, girl. I don't want to scare you, I just want to talk to you. Don't scream."

Eliza nodded her head, her heart beating furiously in her throat. The man pulled her a little further into the alley and then released her. Eliza spun around, her eyes goes wide as she encountered Mr. Dawson – the butcher himself. "Mr. Dawson?!"

He simply shook his head at her and said, "Follow me." He turned and walked down the alley, stepping through a side door that led into the back of his small shop. Eliza was curious, and also a bit angry that he'd manhandled her. She wanted to know his reason, and she followed him, albeit cautiously.

The butcher was a big burly man, and very quiet. She'd known him since she was but a young girl, and while she'd never been afraid of him before, suddenly the rumors surfaced in her mind. Rumors that he used to abuse his wife. The reports had never been proven, and his wife had left him a while back, only making the rumors start up again.

She felt guilty for her thoughts and asked Gott to give her wisdom in dealing with the man. She stepped into his shop and blinked as her eyes adjusted to the dim lighting. "Mr. Dawson?" she called out quietly when she didn't immediately spot him.

"Just a second, I need to find the light switch." She heard his feet shuffling on the concrete, and a moment later bright light had her squinting her eyes as they adjusted once again to the changing light level.

"Sorry to scare you, but I needed to speak with you and I didn't want anyone else to know what I was about."

Eliza nodded her head, "Mr. Dawson, is something wrong?"

"I heard you were looking into the Troyer girl's disappearance?"

Eliza nodded her head, "Ivy was my friend. Thomas Schwartz found her suitcase a few days ago buried down by the river. It was covered in blood, some of which belonged to Ivy according to the police."

"And you want to know what happened to her?" he asked.

"I do. I think her daed and mamm deserve to know what happened to her."

"I agree and I think I can help you with that. What do you know so far?"

Eliza shook her head, "Not much. Ivy saw or overheard something that scared her. Badly. She was afraid to stay here in Millersburg and she left. She told me she was going to live with the Englisch, but she told another friend that she was coming to live with her. She never made it to the friend's haus."

"I think Ivy might have seen my wife and that is what scared her."

"Your wife?"

"My wife and the minister. Minister Miller. I think they might both have had something to do with your friend's disappearance."

Eliza shook her head, "I don't understand. Minister Miller? And your wife?"

"They were having an affair."

"What?" Eliza asked, stumbling back a bit at that news. Minister Miller stood before their Ordnung on a weekly basis and preached Gott's love and things like modesty, purity, and honesty. And this Englischer was now telling her that the man was a fraud and sinner? It was hard to take in.

"I knew of course, but things between me and my wife hadn't been right for a long time, and all we seemed to do was fight. It was my own fault really. I have a temper, and Carrie liked to push my buttons. I used to drink...I don't any longer, but I was a miserable man back then.

"One day, Carrie pushed me when I'd been drinking and I hit her. More than once." He hung his head, tears in his eyes, "I'm not proud of what I did, and I apologized to her over and over, but...she sought refuge at the church with the minister. He became her confidant and friend, and I guess one thing led to another...

"Anyway, I stopped drinking and tried to make things right with my wife, but she and the minister were already having the affair. She continued seeing him, and I felt guilty for hurting her and just turned my attention to other things."

Eliza was stunned. The rumors about Mr. Dawson had been true, but that didn't excuse his fraa's infidelity. Not at all! And Minister Miller...it seemed he took advantage of a hurting fraa who was looking to him for guidance. His actions were inexcusable!

Mr. Dawson continued speaking, "I remember a night about four years ago, I caught her sneaking into the house really late one night, almost early the next morning it was so late.

"She was covered in dirt, her hands caked with it, her shoes and jeans as well. And her shirt…it was covered with bloodstains. They were bright red and unmistakable. I was angry that she'd been out so late at night, but they I thought maybe she'd been injured.

"I followed her to the bathroom and asked her what had happened, and she told me to mind my own business. It was nothing and didn't concern me."

Eliza watched the emotions flow across the mann's face; saw the anger as he clenched his fists. "Was she injured?"

"No! I was so angry with her. We fought and I finally left the house because I was afraid I might end up hurting her. I was more furious with her than I'd ever been before and she wouldn't talk to me. I left the house and went for a long walk. I didn't come back until the sun was already up."

"Did she explain what had happened?" Eliza wanted to know.

"No," he shook his head. "When I returned, she was sleeping. She'd showered and then cleaned the bathroom and the floors, wiping up all of the mud she tracked in. Her soiled clothing was cut up into pieces and thrown in the trash can. She threw her tennis shoes away as well. I asked several times, but she would never discuss it. She was a stubborn woman, and when she got it into her head to do something, she never caved."

"What did you do?" Eliza asked.

"I came to work like I always did. Later that afternoon, I heard the news that Ivy Troyer was missing. I didn't know her, and it was only after I got home later that night and found Carrie had left town, that I began to think there might be a connection between the two events. I thought about going to the police, but the next morning the police announced that she'd left a letter and had simply run away from her Amish upbringing."

"That's what she wanted everyone to think," Eliza told him softly.

Mr. Dawson nodded his head, "When I heard about the suitcase and confirmation that some of the blood on that suitcase belonged to Ivy…well, all of the events from four years ago came rushing back. I certain they are connected."

Eliza was in a daze. If what Mr. Dawson was saying was correct, not only had his wife been involved in Ivy's disappearance, but also Minister Miller!

"I just wanted you to know. Maybe you can figure out a way to set things right for her parents." Mr. Dawson looked sad and Eliza nodded her head and thanked him for sharing his story with her. She exited his shop the same way she'd entered and quickly made her way to the market.

Her mamm was depending on some of the items to prepare a special meal for an upcoming gathering, but Eliza's head wasn't really in the market. It was sorting through the story she'd just heard, and trying to come to terms with the fact that Minister Miller very likely had everything to do with her friend's disappearance. And possibly her death!

The Right Thing to Do

After the weekly worship service…

"Eliza, I was hoping I would see you today," Thomas told her quietly as he joined her after the church service was dismissed.

Eliza smiled and started walking, pleased when he joined her. "I was hoping the same thing. You'll never guess what I've learned."

Thomas gave her a raised brow and she ducked her head as she realized he really was a handsome mann. Dark hair, dark eyes, tall and muscular, but not overly so. His face was still clean shaven, as he was an unmarried mann, and she wondered how he would look with a full beard.

"Did you hear me?" he asked.

She looked up and blushed, realizing she'd been daydreaming and hadn't heard a word he'd said to her. "Sorry." She looked around, making sure that no one was paying them any special attention, especially the minister. "We can't talk here."

"How about I walk with you? I didn't bring the buggy this morning, wanting the exercise."

Eliza nodded and they set off for her haus. "You know Mr. Dawson?"

"The butcher?" When she nodded, he nodded back.

"He spoke with me a few days ago and told me something incredible. He told me his wife was having an affair with Minister Miller."

"What?! Eliza, are you sure? You can't go around saying things like that unless you're certain they are true," he admonished her.

"I know it sounds crazy, but he was telling me the truth. He also told me about a night, the day before Carrie left town, the same night Ivy left Millersburg…"

"What about that night?"

"Carrie came home covered in dirt and blood, but when he questioned her about it, she wouldn't tell him a thing. They fought and he left before he hurt her. He was still really angry with her while he was telling me this."

"Did he know about their affair before this night?" Thomas asked, his voice showing how shocked her was.

"He said he did, but he was tired of fighting with her and had stopped caring."

"That's sad," Thomas commented. "But Minister Miller? He's…"

"I know. He spoke to me the day we got back from Yellowcreek."

"He did? About what?" Thomas wanted to know.

"He told me I needed to stop investigating Ivy's disappearance because it was agitating her parents and other members of the Ordnung."

"Why would he do that? Didn't he want to know what happened to her?" He paused and then his face changed, "Of course he wouldn't! He already knew what happened to her, and with Carrie gone, and Ivy gone…there was no one to uncover his secret. Except for you."

Eliza kicked a rock in the path, "I'm so angry, I don't know what to do! The mann is a murderer, and unless something is done, he's going to get away with it."

"But what can you do? The police know there's at least one other person's blood on the suitcase, but I spoke with Matthew Troyer before the service started, and they haven't been contacted again."

"I don't know yet. I guess I'll give the police a little more time to figure things out, but if they don't, then I'll have to take action myself."

Thomas shook his head, "Eliza be careful. Maybe Mr. Dawson should go to the police and tell them his story? That would keep you out of it."

Eliza nodded her head, "Maybe, but I don't know if he will. I could ask him, I suppose."

"Please do that. I don't want to see anything happen to you. In fact, I was meaning to ask you this today, but would you like to have dinner with me one day soon?"

Eliza felt her heart speed up as she nodded, "I'd like that."

"Gut! I've enjoyed getting to know you and think I'd like to know more about you still."

"I feel the same," Eliza told him, trying to contain the nervous excitement his words evoked. At the age of twenty-two, they were both getting close to the age when people would begin to question why there were still single. They'd both made a choice to remain Amish, and it was expected they would find a life partner and build a life together.

Neither of them had found that special person yet, but Eliza was willing to consider that Thomas might be a good candidate. I need to figure out how to deal with Minister Miller so that I can concentrate on my own future!

"How about Thursday evening?" Thomas asked her.

"That would be fine. I have to deliver produce to the market Thursday afternoon. Shall I just meet you somewhere in town?"

"Ja. I'll pick you up in front of the library around 5 o'clock?" Thomas suggested.

"Wunderbar!" He finished walking her home and she spent the next few days taking care of chores and trying not to let her anger at Minister Miller grow out of proportion. She anxiously awaited news that the police had discovered the identity of the person to whom the blood on the suitcase belonged, but no word came.

By the time Thursday arrived, she was out of patience, and decided to confront Minister Miller with what she knew. If he didn't admit to his actions, she would then go to Mr. Dawson and beg him to tell his story to the police. It was the right thing to do!

Confrontation and Comfort

Thursday afternoon...

Eliza left the market and headed towards the church. There were still two hours before she was supposed to meet Thomas outside the library, and she found herself unable to avoid confronting the minister any longer.

She stepped inside the church, and looked around for him. He wasn't immediately visible, so she called out, "Minister Miller?"

"Be right there. Have a seat."

Eliza took a seat on the back pew, Thomas's warning about being careful echoing in her head. She was just starting to think that maybe she should have brought him along when she had this confrontation, but before she could get up to leave, Minister Miller was standing there in front of her.

"Elizabeth. What are you doing here?" he asked in a cold voice.

Eliza stood up and then answered him, "I know everything. Mr. Dawson talked to me last week."

Minister Miller paled and she noticed his hands were trembling slightly as he stuck them into the pockets of his suit jacket. He was as white as a ghost, but his next words belied his physical reaction.

"I don't know what that evil Englischer could have to say to you of any importance."

"He told me about your affair with his wife." Eliza folded her arms across one another, staring him down and trying not to show how nervous this conversation was making her.

Minister Miller blanched even whiter, if that were possible, and then shook his head, "He's lying." He turned and stalked towards the front of the church building. Eliza followed him.

"He also told me that Carrie came home one night covered in mud and that she had bloodstains all over her shirt. He seems to think that you and Carrie might have had something to do with Ivy's disappearance."

 When the minister didn't say anything, she continued, "Did she see you with Carrie Dawson? Is that why scared her so much she felt like she needed to leave Millersburg? What would the Ordnung and elders think if they knew of your infidelity?" she challenged him.

She was unprepared when he bent over a small wooden desk and then turned with a pistol in his hand. "The elders will never find out. How dare you threaten me! You're nothing but a stupid girl who doesn't know when to keep her nose out of other people's business."

Eliza stared at the gun, her throat closing up in fear. "I…"

"Your friend was an unfortunate accident. She wandered behind the old abandoned barn a few miles out of town and caught Carrie and I in the middle of a passionate embrace. She was shocked and might have been able to run away, without either of knowing she'd been there, but she tripped over an old board in her haste to get away.

"I chased after her and she tried to tell me she'd seen nothing, but I could tell she was lying. I threatened her to keep her mouth shut and not tell anybody. My reputation was at stake…"

"Maybe you should have considered that before you decided to sleep with another mann's fraa,' Eliza accused him, keeping her eyes on the gun.

"What do you know? I control this village. Everyone sees me as being virtuous…"

"And pious and domineering…have I missed anything?" Eliza challenged him again.

"Watch your mouth! This village respects me and admired me for my dedication and faith. When you show up missing, everyone will be suitably upset and I will comfort them the best I can. In a month, everything will be back to normal and no one will ever be the wiser.

"Your friend would still be alive if she'd heeded my warning."

"What do you mean, still alive? Did you kill her?" Eliza asked, wishing there was someone else to hear this evil mann's confession.

"I saw her leave your house that last night. She had a suitcase in her hands and I was sure she'd told you everything. I couldn't let her tell anyone else. I grabbed her when she stepped into the trees and hit her on the head. I dragged her down by the river and stabbed her."

Eliza felt her stomach turn over as she listened to the mann she'd known since she could remember talk so calmly about killing another human being. Her best friend, Ivy. "You didn't have to kill her; she didn't tell me anything."

"I know that now, but I couldn't take any chances. I was angry that she had gone against my orders and reacted out of rage. And now, you will also suffer the same fate."

"I don't think so," came a loud male voice from behind Eliza.

She turned her head, amazed to see three uniformed police officers standing in the doorway to the church, their pistols drawn and pointed directly at the minister.

"Young lady, come back here please."

Eliza started to obey them, but Minister Miller wasn't convinced his game was up yet. "If you move, I'll shoot you."

Eliza froze, unsure of what she should do. The decision was made for her a moment later when another uniformed officer burst through the side door of the church building and tackled the minister to the ground, knocking the pistol from his hands in the process.

Eliza turned and sprinted up the aisle between the pews, "He killed Ivy Troyer. He just told me…"

"We know, we heard it all. We were coming here to question him about the lab finding his blood on the suitcase when we overheard his confession." The officer gave her arm a quick squeeze and then strode to the front of the building where a very angry Minister Miller was being handcuffed while lying on the floorboards on his stomach.

"You can't do this, I'm a Minister!"

"You are a murderer." The officer proceeded to read him his rights as another officer led Eliza out of the building. She sat down on the steps and gave the woman police officer a statement and was just finishing up when Thomas came running across the street.

"Eliza! What's happened?"

She gave him a sad smile, "Minister Miller is being arrested for Ivy's murder. He admitted the entire thing to me…"

Thomas stepped forward and placed a hand on her arm. She felt a tingly sensation rush through her body, but they were surrounded by police officers and other townspeople who had noticed the activity around the church.

"I'll need you to come to the station and give a more formal station, but you're free to go now."

Eliza thanked the officer and allowed Thomas to lead her to where he'd parked his buggy. "I can't believe he killed her."

"Are you alright?" he asked, concern in his voice after he handed her up into the buggy.

"I think so. He pulled a pistol out and was going to shoot me!" she said, just before she burst into tears.

Thomas stepped into the space left by the opened buggy door and gingerly hugged her, "It's okay, nothing happened."

"I know, I'm not sure why I'm crying," she told him as she tried to gain control of her emotions once more.

"You had a shock, it's okay to be upset."

"I need to go speak to the Troyer's. They deserve to know what happened."

Thomas looked at her and then asked, "Would you like some company?"

Eliza nodded and gave him a smile, "I would really like some company. Danke."

Thomas searched her eyes for a moment and then nodded his head once, "You are very welcome. Let's get this behind us and then I would like to try dinner once again and see if maybe we might have more than friendship between us. I like you, Eliza. A lot."

"I like you to. I'm ready to put this all behind us." And I can't wait until we finally are able to have our dinner together. I've never felt like I do right now after receiving a hug. That has to mean something.

Epilogue

One week later…

Thomas and Eliza left the police station and headed back to Millersburg. Thomas had just finished giving his final statement to the police, and Eliza had identified the remains of her friend from the pictures the police had shown her.

She'd offered to do the task so that the Troyer's wouldn't have to. It had been one of the hardest things she'd ever done, but having Thomas standing by her side had given her the help she needed.

After the police had arrested Minister Miller, they'd taken him back to the station and he'd given them a full confession. They'd identified his blood from samples stored in the state database. They'd been trying to piece his involvement together, when Mr. Dawson had paid them a visit. He'd told them what he knew and they started a hunt for Carrie Dawson.

They hadn't found her yet, and it appeared the woman had changed her name after leaving Millersburg. The chances that they would ever find her and make her accountable for her part in Ivy's death was slim. She'd not been involved in the actual murder, but when Minister Miller had shown up at her haus that night and asked for her help, she'd gone with him and helped him bury the body and suitcase.

The police found Ivy's decomposed body buried five feet from where Thomas had found the suitcase. The coroner had confirmed that she died from stab wounds, and Minister Miller was being charged with her murder and would stand trial in an Englisch courtroom to answer for his crimes.

The small Ordnung had been shocked to hear the details of his affair and the extent he'd been willing to go to cover up his sins. For Eliza, identifying Ivy's body was bittersweet. She was sad for the way Ivy's life had ended, but also happy that her daed and mamm would finally have a chance to give the dochder a proper burial.

"Did you get a chance to review Minister Miller's confession?" Thomas asked Eliza when they were headed back to Millersburg.

"I did. He was always so condescending to everyone, reminding the people that they were sinners and needed to repent. I guess he thought he was superior to everyone else. He told the police he'd been planning to end his affair with Carrie, but just hadn't been able to find the willpower to do so."

"He also told them that he hadn't intended to hurt Ivy, but he was afraid word of his infidelity would get out. The people feared and respected him and he wanted to protect that at all costs," Thomas added.

"Do you remember how upset he seemed when word started circulating that Mr. Dawson was abusing his wife? He was so angry, and yet his own anger caused him to kill Ivy."

"I think that's called irony. I'm just relieved that this is all behind us now No more questions to answer, and once the funeral is over, maybe things can get back to normal."

"Normal? It doesn't seem like things have been normal for a while now."

Thomas glanced at her and then slowed the buggy down, "I have a suggestion for how to start getting back to normal. Would you like to hear it?"

Eliza looked at him and smiled, "Sure."

"Well, how about we stop at the diner and ask Fraa Hochstedler to pack us a picnic lunch and drive to the river and eat it together? Not the part of the river where all of this took place, but that little grassy knoll that overlooks the roller dam."

Eliza sighed, "That sounds very normal and I would love to accompany you."

Thomas smiled at her and then gingerly reached over and took her hand in his own, "Is this okay?"

Eliza squeezed his hand in return, "It's more than okay."

Thomas held her hand the entire way back to Millersburg, and as they walked to the grassy knoll where they had their picnic together. Eliza and he spent a carefree afternoon, talking about everything except Ivy's murder.

They found they shared the same dreams and hopes for the future, and as he handed her down from his buggy several hours later in from of her familye's haus, he kissed her for the first time. Sealing their future together.

They'd not only helped solve the questions surrounding a missing Amish girl and friend, but they'd found each other in the process. What had started out as horrible discovery had found a happy ending for them, and a bittersweet closure for everyone who'd known Ivy Troyer. Her murderer would be held accountable, the Troyer's would finally be allowed to heal, and he and Eliza would get married, have several children, and live a full and productive life. Together.

About the Author

By signing up to Hannah Schrock's mailing list you will be the very first to hear about all of her new releases. Members of her mailing list always get the lowest possible price on new books PLUS you will also get occasional FREE Amish stories.

Click Here to add your email address!

I would like to thank you for taking the time to download my book. I really hope that you enjoyed it as much as I enjoyed writing it.

If you feel able I would love for you to give the book a short review on Amazon.

If you want to keep up to date with all of my latest releases then please like my FACEBOOK PAGE

Many thanks once again, all my love.

Hannah.

LATEST BOOKS

DON'T MISS HANNAH'S BRAND NEW MAMMOTH AMISH MEGA BOOK - 20 Stories in one box set.

Mammoth Amish Romance Mega Book 20 books in one set

Also out

Amish Mystery and Romance Box Set – 6 Books

MOST RECENT SINGLE TITLES

The Amish Wallflower
The Orphan's Amish Teacher
The Mysterious Amish Suicide
The Pregnant Amish Quilt Maker
The Amish Caregiver
The Amish Detective: The King Family Arsonist

Hannah Schrock is the author of over 50 Amish titles. View the full list **HERE**

A Taster

Also out Now by Hannah Schrock...

The Amish Wallflower

Here is a Taster...

September, Somerset County, Pennsylvania...

"Mary? Where are you?" Samuel Hertzler called out into the shadows of the barn. The sun was already rising high in the sky and his dochder should have been finished with her morning chores hours ago.

He'd already looked for her in the haus, only to find it empty. The morning dishes had been washed and were drying in the rack next to the sink, and the floorboards on the porch were still damp – evidence that Mary had scrubbed them recently.

He'd thought she might be tending to the garden, or the flower beds behind the haus, but she'd been in neither place. He turned from the entrance to the barn with an apologetic smile for his guests, "It seems she is off tending to other chores. Why don't we go sit in the cool of the porch while we wait?"

The two men nodded their heads and followed him back to the porch, taking seats in the wooden chairs and enjoying the respite from the hot sun. It was late August, and the temperatures hadn't yet shown signs of Fall's arrival.

"Your dochder often disappears during the day?" Mr. Amman inquired politely, a note of censure in his voice in regards to the missing young woman. The man was a recent member of their Ordnung and didn't know his dochder or her reputation. Her own community was well aware of her predilection to stay off by herself when in a large group.

"Nee. Mary is a gut dochder, just a bit shy where strangers are concerned." He silently asked Gott to forgive his slight exaggeration. In reality, Mary was extremely shy. She was the spitting image of her Mamm, Gott rest her soul, but only in looks.

Her Mamm had died giving birth to their second child when Mary was merely five years old. The babe had died as well, leaving Mary without a mamm and her daed without a fraa. The community had gathered around the grieving minister and his young dochder, but the ensuing years had been difficult. He'd often asked Gott if staying a widow had been the best thing for himself and Mary.

As the only minister in their small Ordnung for the last ten years, it was his responsibility to help shepherd and minister to the community. His job was made slightly easier in that this particular Ordnung was unique in the way Sunday services were handled.

In most Ordnung, a different family would host the Sunday services at their home. Because of the amount of work this required, meetings would be held once a month, or maybe every other week. Families would hold their own Sunday meetings amongst themselves on the off weeks.

But in Somerset County, this Amish Ordnung wanted to worship weekly, so a meeting house had been constructed years earlier and now all Sunday services were held there. Weekly. Samuel Hertzler had come to this Ordnung as a young married man to learn from the older minister who hoped one day to turn the Ordnung's spiritual shepherding over to someone else.

Samuel felt blessed to have been able to work alongside Mr. Fisher for more than a decade, and while he still had days where he felt inadequate to the task before him, he also knew that he should put his trust in Gott and no one else. Least of all himself.

He nodded to the two men and then walked to the edge of the porch, looking out into the fields beyond. He was relieved when he saw Mary coming towards home, a basket of flowers in her arms.

Mary had recently taken up the task of making sure there were fresh flowers on the eating tables, where the entire community took a meal together, after the weekly worship services. That wasn't always possible, given the changing of the seasons, but whenever possible, she trekked through the fields, or harvested blooms from her own garden to place upon the tables. When Samuel had asked her about it, she'd smiled and told him she liked seeing the beauty that Gott created displayed.

He'd been hard pressed to argue against the small decoration, himself loving to take a walk through the fields and the surrounding countryside, the sole purpose being to admire Gott's handiwork. He often recited the

Psalms while doing so, in German or course, and any Englisch passing by would have deemed him crazy for talking to himself.

He didn't really mind, his conversations with Gott were an ongoing thing, and he was happy to say that his dochder seemed to have picked up the habit as well. It wasn't unusual to find her holding a murmured conversation with the garden plants, or the farm animals. If only she could speak to other people as easily.

He waited until she was within earshot and then called to her, "Mary. I need you here."

She lifted her head, her mind somewhere else, and smiled at him with a wave. He knew the minute she realized they had company because the smile upon her face froze and her stance faltered. He wished there was a way he could help her overcome her fear of being around people, but after years of trying, he'd decided it was all in Gott's hands now.

"Mary is coming now," he informed the two men. Mr. Amman was the son of one of the oldest families in the Ordnung and with him today, was Mr. Faye. Both men sat on the elder council and had come to see Samuel today in regards to an Englischer that had just requested to join their Ordnung.

It wasn't a usual request, but Samuel had no problem with allowing this young man to seek Gott amongst them. He'd personally met with this mann and found him to be hurting and searching for the truth. There was no better place to do so than in an Amish community in Samuel's opinion.

The men's visit today also had another purpose. Mary was a master quilter and sold her wares in a small store in the middle of town. The Englisch loved buying textiles and furniture, and Mary's quilts never stayed in the store very long before they were sold.

Mr. Amman had taken over running the family store, and had received a very unusual request from an Englischer late yesterday afternoon. It seemed this individual owned a camp of some sort and required quilts for each of the beds in the small tourist cabins. A total of eight quilts was a large order and would take many months to complete, but the man hadn't been swayed.

There had only been one stipulation, and that was the reason Mr. Amman was currently waiting to speak with his dochder. The Englischer wanted all of the quilts made by her, using a very distinctive pattern that only she used in their Ordnung. He wanted them in a variety of colors and textures, but all in the same exact design.

"Daed, you wanted to see me?" Mary spoke very quietly from the bottom of the stairs.

Samuel nodded and then waved her forward, "Mr. Amman is here to tell you about an order he received today."

Mary nodded her head and then looked at the older gentleman, "Mr. Amman."

"Mary, I have an order for eight of your quilts. How long do you think it will take to make that many?"

"Eight?" she asked timidly. Her face showed her surprise.

"Jah. I know that is a lot, but the Englischer assured me he is in no hurry. So, how long?"

Mary shook her head, "I truly don't know. I have one almost ready to finish…"

Mr. Amman shook his head, "He wants them all done like the Blue and Green Carpenter's Wheel quilt you brought in two weeks ago."

Mary nodded her head, "It will take a while…"

"He knows that. This Englischer understands patience. He'll be back in a month to pay for and pick up whatever you have finished."

Mary nodded and then turned to her Daed, "Was there something else you needed?"

Samuel looked at his dochder and nodded his head, "I will be going to see the Shepard's in half an hour. You will be coming with me." He could see that she wanted to argue and protest, but he also knew that she would not dare to do so in front of their guests.

She hated being forced to accompany him on his visits around the community, but he took every opportunity to put her in situations where she would be forced to socialize. Her timid nature was befuddling to him, and this was his way of dealing with it. She might dislike the chore right now, but hopefully, somewhere in the future, she would reap the benefits.

Mary sat on a bale of hay in the barn, her heart racing and her breath coming raggedly as she thought about accompanying her father this afternoon. He knew she disliked having to make small talk with the Fraas and kinner while he visited with the menner of the haus.

They usually wanted to talk about chores, her quilts, or the upcoming wedding season and which boy was most likely to marry which girl. It wasn't that she wasn't interested in the information, she just didn't want to have to actively participate in the discussion.

Since she was around eight years old, she found it hard to talk to more than one person at a time. At times, her fears had become so overwhelming, she'd had a panic attack, requiring her father to cut short his visit and see her home.

He usually explained her little incidents away by making it appear as if she were suddenly taken ill, but he knew the truth. And most of her fellow community members knew the truth as well. The other young women around her age found it a good source of gossip. The Amish weren't a people given to discussing others' shortcomings, but her peer group was immature and what their parents didn't know, couldn't be corrected. More than once, she'd wandered past a group of her peers only to hear them whispering and laughing about her.

"Mary, I'm ready to go," her daed called into the barn a few minutes later.

"Coming, Daed," she called out, standing up and automatically dusting off her skirts and patting the kapp covering her hair. Her long brown hair was braided around her head and twisted up beneath the white cap, and a black apron covered her dark blue dress. Black stockings covered her calves, and the black leather shoes were still clean and polished, even after her morning walk through the fields.

She exited the barn and then carefully climbed into the black buggy, mentally preparing herself for the rest of the afternoon. The Shepard's were a very large family, and Anna had just given birth to her seventh child. Their oldest dochder was about the same age as Mary, but the two young women had never been what anyone would call friends.

Sara Jane was a very outgoing young woman, and Mary had spent many Sunday afternoons, watching her and the other young people socialize. Laughter and obvious enjoyment of the singing and games that were offered after each lengthy worship service was very apparent amongst her peers, but Mary never participated directly.

Mary rarely even engaged in their conversations, choosing instead to busy herself with straightening the food tables, or sitting quietly against the barn wall, a silent observer to the gaiety going on around her.

"Mary?"

She jerked slightly, turning her head to see her daed looking at her with concern. "Sorry, I guess my mind wandered a bit."

"I was reminding you that the young people will be having their harvest celebration tomorrow after the worship service. There is a young man, an Englischer, that has joined us. I want you to make him feel welcome."

"What?" she asked, perplexed.

"Jah, the elder council accepted his request to join the faith a fortnight ago. He has purchased a small property at the edge of town and has chosen to abandon his Englisch ways for our own."

"He is to be baptized?" she asked curiously.

"Jah. In October. I will introduce you to him tomorrow."

Mary blanched, "That is not necessary. Maybe you could speak with Sara Jane..."

"Nee. You are my dochder and it is only fitting that you should make his acquaintance."

Mary nodded agreeably, inside shaking with fear. She barely spoke to the other young women, and almost never to the young men. The other girls were always whispering about her, and not necessarily behind her back. She knew they thought she was a freak because she rarely spoke to anyone else outside her immediate family.

Her aunts and uncles and their children were used to her shyness, and rather than push her into a panic, they usually just nodded a greeting to her and let her be. Her father was another story though. He seemed bent on making her a social butterfly and every time he forced her to interact with the other young people, she felt a sense of panic that was often hard to handle.

They arrived at the Shepard haus and she immediately was surrounded by the younger children who were intent on showing her the newest litter of kittens in the barn. The younger children didn't mind if she didn't say a whole lot, and she looked to her daed for permission, relieved when he gave her a nod of assent.

She could dawdle in the barn for a while, and hopefully he would be ready to leave when she finally reached the haus. That was much preferred over having to answer questions from Sara Jane or her mamm. Much preferred.

*****

That evening as Mary readied herself for bed, she couldn't quit thinking about the introduction her daed intended to make the next afternoon. The only thing that kept her from going into a full blown panic attack at the thought was wanting to find out why an Englischer would want to become Amish.

She immediately felt guilty for the thoughts she often had whilst in the town delivery her quilts. There was a bench situated a short distance from Mr. Amman's shop, and she would oftentimes sit on it, watching the Englisch go to and fro in their motorized vehicles, their unusual clothing, and the casual way they interacted with one another.

Since becoming a teenager, she had always been fascinated by their lifestyle. She often marveled at their ways and how simple some tasks must be for them. She'd even imagined herself leaving the Amish community and living amongst them, more than once.

When it came time for her Rumspringa, she'd toyed with the idea of partaking of that world for a season, but her shyness and inability to socialize like other girls her age had proven to be too much to overcome. She'd stayed home, making her daed smile with joy, while inside she longed to experience that other world. But feelings of guilt always accompanied such thoughts and she would push them aside.

And now one of them had come to live amongst the Amish she called her own. A young mann who had grown up in that other world. A mann who was used to the modern conveniences the Amish refused to partake in.

Why? What would make a mann leave that world for this one? Maybe I can find enough courage to ask?

The Amish Wallflower

Made in the USA
Las Vegas, NV
09 April 2023

70400237R00049